PowerKids Readers:

The Bilingual Library of the United States of America™

Bilingual Edition
English / Spanish
Edición bilingüe

HAWAII
HAWAI

JOSÉ MARÍA OBREGÓN

TRADUCCIÓN AL ESPAÑOL: MARÍA CRISTINA BRUSCA

The Rosen Publishing Group's
PowerKids Press™ & **Editorial Buenas Letras**™
New York

Published in 2005 by The Rosen Publishing Group, Inc.
29 East 21st Street, New York, NY 10010

First Edition

Photo Credits: Cover © Tomas del Amo/Index Stock Imagery, Inc.; p. 5 © Joe Sohm/The Image Works; p. 7 © 2002 Geoatlas; pp. 9, 11, 23, 31 (Volcano) © Michael T. Sedam/Corbis; pp. 13, 31 (Kahanamoku) © Getty Images; pp. 15, 31 (Kamehameha I) © Time Life Pictures/Getty Images; pp. 17, 19, 31 (Ariyoshi, Ho, Army Base, Attack, Surf) © Bettmann/Corbis; p. 21 © Catherine Karnow/Corbis; pp. 25, 30 (Capital) © Richard Cummins/Corbis; pp. 26, 30 (The Aloha State) © Jean Mele/Corbis; p. 30 (Yellow Hibiscus) © Dave G. Houser/Corbis; p. 30 (Hawaiian Goose) © Francesc Muntada/Corbis; p. 30 (Kukui/Candlenut) © Douglas Peebles/Corbis; p. 31 (Liliuokalani) © Rykoff Collection/Corbis; p. 31 (Carrere) © Mitchell Gerber/Corbis

Library of Congress Cataloging-in-Publication Data

Obregón, José María, 1963–
Hawaii / José María Obregón ; traducción al español, María Cristina Brusca.— 1st ed.
p. cm. — (The bilingual library of the United States of America) Includes bibliographical references and index. ISBN 1-4042-3076-9 (library binding)
1. Hawaii—Juvenile literature. I. Title. II. Series.

DU623.25.O27 2005
996.9-dc22

2005001248

Manufactured in the United States of America

Due to the changing nature of Internet links, Editorial Buenas Letras has developed an online list of Web sites related to the subject of this book. This site is updated regularly. Please use this link to access the list:

http://www.buenasletraslinks.com/ls/hawaii

Contents

Contenido

Welcome to Hawaii

Hawaii is known as the Aloha State. In the Hawaiian language, "aloha" means both hello and goodbye.

Bienvenidos a Hawai

Hawái es conocido como el Estado Aloha. En el idioma hawaiano "aloha" significa hola y también significa adiós.

The Flag and Seal of the State of Hawaii

Bandera y escudo de Hawái

Hawaii Geography

Hawaii is a group of 137 volcanic islands in the central Pacific Ocean. There are eight main islands, Hawaii, Kahoolawe, Kauai, Lanai, Molokai, Niihau, Oahu, and Maui.

Geografía de Hawai

Hawai es un grupo de 137 islas volcánicas que están en el Océano Pacífico central. Las ocho islas mayores son Hawai, Kahoolawe, Kauai, Lanai, Molokai, Niihau, Oahu y Maui.

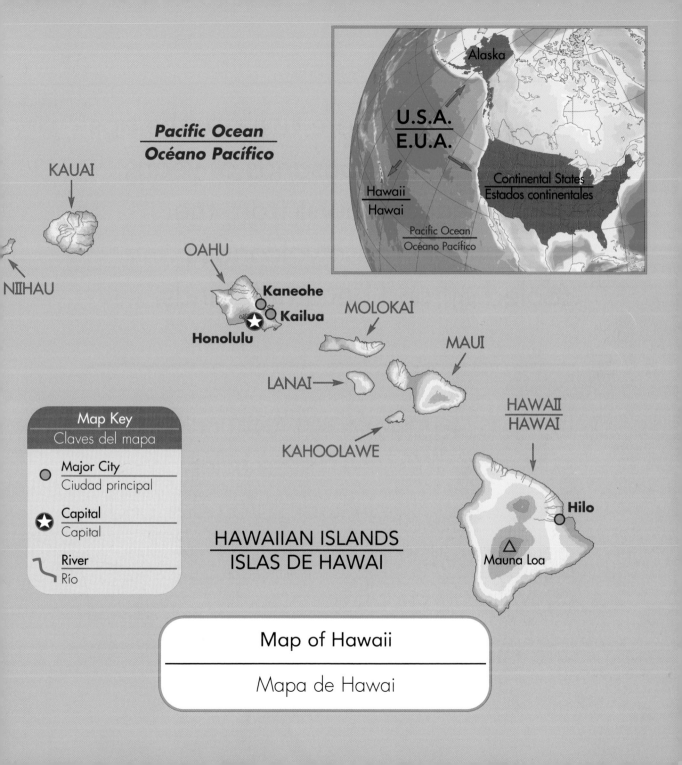

Pacific Ocean
Océano Pacífico

KAUAI

NIIHAU

OAHU

Kaneohe

Kailua

Honolulu

MOLOKAI

LANAI

MAUI

KAHOOLAWE

HAWAII
HAWAI

Hilo

Mauna Loa

U.S.A.
E.U.A.

Alaska

Continental States
Estados continentales

Hawaii
Hawai

Pacific Ocean
Océano Pacífico

Map Key
Claves del mapa

○ Major City
Ciudad principal

★ Capital
Capital

〰 River
Río

HAWAIIAN ISLANDS
ISLAS DE HAWAI

Map of Hawaii

Mapa de Hawai

Hawaii's islands are actually the tips of volcanoes. Thousands of years ago, volcanoes burst from the ocean floor. These volcanoes cooled off and became islands.

Las islas de Hawái son realmente las puntas de volcanes. Hace miles de años, estos volcanes brotaron del fondo del mar. Cuando se enfriaron, se convirtieron en islas.

View of the Island of Oahu

Vista de la isla Oahu

Hawaii History

Polynesian settlers were the first to arrive in Hawaii. They arrived 1,500 years ago in boats. The Polynesians built communities on the eight major islands.

Historia de Hawai

Los polinesios fueron los primeros en establecerse en Hawai. Llegaron en canoas hace 1,500 años. Los polinesios construyeron poblados en las ocho islas mayores.

Polynesian Settlers Built Totems

Los pobladores polinesios construyeron totems

English explorer Captain James Cook arrived in Hawaii in 1778. He claimed the islands for Britain and named them the Sandwich Islands. The name did not last long.

Un explorador inglés, el Capitán James Cook, llegó a Hawai en 1778. Cook reclamó las islas para Gran Bretaña y las nombró Islas Sandwich. Ese nombre no duró mucho tiempo.

English Explorer Captain James Cook

El capitán James Cook, explorador inglés

Many years ago Hawaii was ruled by kings. King Kamehameha I was born in North Kohala on the island of Hawaii. King Kamehameha I governed the islands from 1785 to 1810.

Hace muchos años Hawai era gobernado por reyes. El rey Kamehameha I nació en North Kohala, en la isla de Hawai. El rey Kamehameha I gobernó las islas desde 1785 hasta 1810.

King Kamehameha I of Hawaii

Rey Kamehameha I de Hawai

In December 1941, the Japanese army attacked Pearl Harbor, a navy base near Honolulu. The attack brought the United States into World War II. This war was fought in Europe and Asia.

En diciembre de 1941, la aviación japonesa atacó Pearl Harbor, una base naval americana cerca de Honolulú. Debido a este ataque los Estados Unidos entraron en la Segunda Guerra Mundial. Esta guerra se desarrolló en Europa y Asia.

Battleships Burning at Pearl Harbor

Barcos de guerra se queman en Pearl Harbor

Living in Hawaii

In the Hawaiian language the word *he'e nalu* means "to slide on a wave," or "to surf." Hawaiians have been riding the waves since the eighth century.

La vida en Hawai

En el idioma hawaiano la palabra *he'e nalu* significa "deslizarse en una ola" o "hacer surf". Los hawaianos se han deslizado sobre las olas desde el siglo octavo.

Hawaiian Natives Surfing

Nativos hawaianos haciendo surf

Hawaiians are a mixed group of people. The islands are home to many people of Japanese, Filipino, Chinese, and Portuguese origin. Hawaii is the most diverse state in America.

La sociedad hawaiana es mixta. Las islas son el hogar de muchas personas de origen japonés, filipino, chino y portugués. Hawai es el estado más diverso de América.

Hawaiian Children

Niños hawaianos

Hawaii Today

Millions of visitors enjoy Hawaii every year. So many visitors can be a problem for the islands. Hawaiians want to keep the beauty of their land and still be a friendly state for visitors.

Hawai, hoy

Cada año, millones de turistas disfrutan de Hawai. Tantos visitantes pueden crear problemas para las islas. Los hawaianos quieren conservar la belleza de su tierra y seguir siendo un estado amigable con sus visitantes.

Visitors Enjoying Waikiki Beach
Visitantes disfrutan de la playa Waikiki

Honolulu, Hilo, and Kailua are
important cities in Hawaii.
Honolulu is the capital of Hawaii.

Honolulú, Hilo y Kailua son
ciudades importantes de Hawai.
Honolulú es la capital de Hawai.

Hawaii's State Capitol Building in Honolulu

Capitolio del estado de Hawai en Honolulú

Activity:
Let's Draw a Hawaiian Lei
Leis are necklaces made of flowers that Hawaiians use to say "aloha" to visitors.

Actividad:
Dibujemos un *lei* hawaiano
Un lei es un collar de flores que los hawaianos usan para decir "aloha" a los visitantes.

1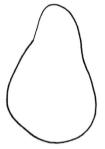

Start by drawing the shape of the necklace.

Comienza por dibujar la forma del collar.

Then start to add small circles along the shape you drew in step 1.

2

Ahora agrega pequeños círculos a lo largo de la figura que dibujaste en el paso número uno.

26

3

Add flower petals between the circles, using S-shaped lines.

Agrega pétalos de flores entre los círculos, usando líneas en forma de S.

4

Add detail to your petals. Short, straight lines will do.

Agrega detalles a los pétalos mediante trazos rectos y cortos.

5

Add shading to your lei, and you are done!

¡Sombrea tu *lei* y habrás terminado!

Timeline

Cronología

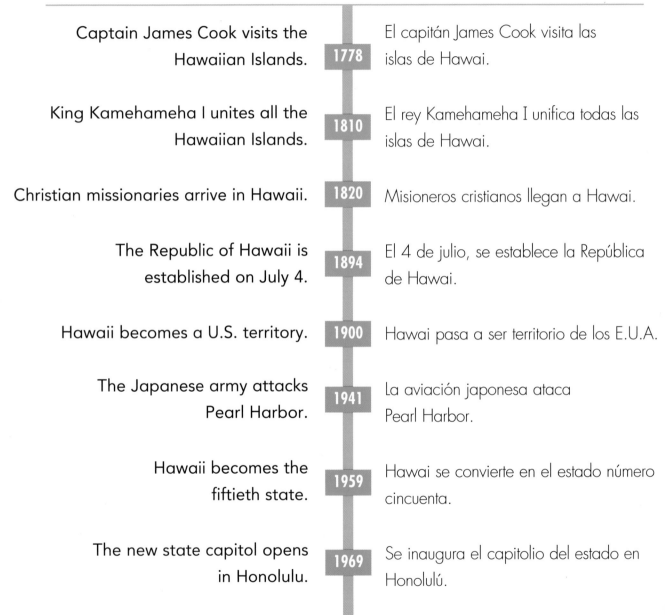

Timeline		Cronología
Captain James Cook visits the Hawaiian Islands.	**1778**	El capitán James Cook visita las islas de Hawai.
King Kamehameha I unites all the Hawaiian Islands.	**1810**	El rey Kamehameha I unifica todas las islas de Hawai.
Christian missionaries arrive in Hawaii.	**1820**	Misioneros cristianos llegan a Hawai.
The Republic of Hawaii is established on July 4.	**1894**	El 4 de julio, se establece la República de Hawai.
Hawaii becomes a U.S. territory.	**1900**	Hawai pasa a ser territorio de los E.U.A.
The Japanese army attacks Pearl Harbor.	**1941**	La aviación japonesa ataca Pearl Harbor.
Hawaii becomes the fiftieth state.	**1959**	Hawai se convierte en el estado número cincuenta.
The new state capitol opens in Honolulu.	**1969**	Se inaugura el capitolio del estado en Honolulú.

Hawaii Events

January
ula Bowl all-star football game on O'ahu
Narcissus Festival in Honolulu

February–March
Cherry Blossom Festival in Honolulu

April
Ching Ming (Chinese cleaning and
epairing ancestral grave sites), statewide

May
Lei Day, statewide
50th State Fair on Oahu (Through June)

June
ng Kamehameha I celebration, statewide

August
apanese Bon Dances at Buddhist centers
Prince Lot Hula Festival, in Honolulu

November
Kona Coffee Festival on Hawaii Island

Eventos en Hawái

Enero
Partido de las estrellas del fútbol
americano Hula Bowl, en Oahu
Festival del narciso, en Honolulú

Febrero-marzo
Festival del pimpollo del cerezo,
en Honolulú

Abril
Ching Ming (limpieza y reparación
de las tumbas ancestrales chinas),
en todo el estado

Mayo
Día del lei, en todo el estado
Feria del Estado Cincuenta , en Oahu
(hasta junio)

Junio
Celebración del rey Kamehameha I, en
todo el estado

Agosto
Danzas japonesas Bon en los centros
budistas
Festival Hula del príncipe Lot, en Honolulú

Noviembre
Festival del café Kona, en isla Hawai

Hawaii Facts/Datos sobre Hawai

<u>Population</u> 1.2 million		<u>Población</u> 1.2 millones
<u>Capital</u> Honolulu		<u>Capital</u> Honolulú
<u>State Motto</u> The Life of the Land is Perpetuated in Righteousness		<u>Lema del estado</u> La vida de la tierra se perpetúa en el respeto
<u>State Flower</u> Yellow Hibiscus		<u>Flor del estado</u> Hibisco amarillo
<u>State Bird</u> Hawaiian Goose (Nene)		<u>Ave del estado</u> Ganso hawaiano (nene)
<u>State Nickname</u> The Aloha State		<u>Mote del estado</u> El Estado Aloha
<u>State Tree</u> Kukui (candlenut)		<u>Árbol del estado</u> Kukui (Nuez de candela)

Famous Hawaiians/Hawaianos famosos

Kamehameha I
(1758?–1819)

King of Hawaii
Rey de Hawai

Liliuokalani
(1838–1917)

Queen of Hawaii
Reina de Hawai

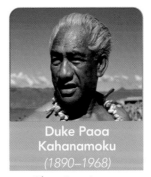

Duke Paoa Kahanamoku
(1890–1968)

Olympic swimmer
Nadador olímpico

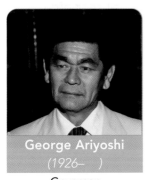

George Ariyoshi
(1926–)

Governor
Gobernador

Don Ho
(1930–)

Singer
Cantante

Tia Carrere
(1967–)

Actress
Actriz

Words to Know/Palabras que debes saber

attack
ataque

navy base
base naval

surf

volcano
volcán

Here are more books to read about Hawaii:
Otros libros que puedes leer sobre Hawái:

In English/En inglés:

Hawaii (From Sea to Shining Sea)
by P. J. Neri
Childrens Press, 2003

Hawaii (Hello U.S.A.)
by Johnston, Joyce
Lerner Publishers, 2001

Words in English: 289

Palabras en español: 303

Index

Índice